Believing
is the
Beginning

The
Caring
Cloud

and

The
Flutterby

Two Children's Stories by Jed Griswold
Illustrations by Jerry Aissis

Copyright © 2022, 2023 by Jed Griswold

ISBN: 978-1-959957-28-7 (Paperback)
ISBN: 978-1-959957-29-4 (Hard Cover)

Original story by Jed Griswold
Format, design and editing by Jed Griswold
Original watercolor illustrations by Jerry Aissis

About the Author

Dr. Jed Griswold is a published author, a retired college administrator and Professor of Psychology, a retired minister, and currently an educational and organizational consultant living in New England.
info@griswoldconsulting.net or visit
www.griswoldconsulting.net

About the Illustrator

Jerry Aissis is a retired teacher who is known for bright and bold colors in his landscapes and seascapes. He teaches art classes and displays his artwork in many New England venues. "There is inspiration all around you. Never stop looking. Never stop painting." Visit
https://FineArtAmerica.com

Also by this Author

A Great Retirement, Griswold Consulting
Climby the Caterpillar, Griswold Consulting
Always Dream Big, Griswold Consulting
In Between, Griswold Consulting
Finding Beauty, Griswold Consulting
Finding My Groups, Griswold Consulting
Finding Myself by Finding Others, Griswold Consulting
Growing Up Through Changes and Challenges, Griswold Consulting
Leafy the Leaf, Griswold Consulting
The Flutterby, Griswold Consulting
The Little Drop of Water, Griswold Consulting
The Power of Storytelling, Wood Lake Publishing
Smally the Seed, Griswold Consulting
Who Haunts This House? Griswold Consulting

The Caring Cloud

Story by Jed Griswold

Illustrations by Jerry Aissis

Once upon a time,
there lived
a caring cloud

who loved
to watch over
all creatures
everywhere.

The Caring Cloud
watched over
creatures tall
and small,

Including
butterflies
and birds.

The caring cloud
smiled when listening
to every tweet
from creatures
with wings
who were near
and far.

The Caring Cloud
knew
that everyone
on earth

had a very
special worth.

Including
those who live
high above the earth,
or in the middle,
or low to the ground,
or even hidden
under oceans
or under the ground,

like
whales
and worms,

waves
and wind,

and even
trees and bees.

The creatures
of skies,
land,
and oceans
could usually see
the Caring Cloud,

and they
were happy
when it was
shading the sun,
or providing rain
for gardens,
or even
preventing
some snow
to grow.

But there was
a problem.

Sometimes
the creatures
of skies,
land
and oceans
could not see
the Caring Cloud.

which made them
worry
that the cloud
and its caring
had left them
alone.

The Caring Cloud
wondered,
"How can I remind
the creatures
of earth
that I am
always caring,
even if
I can't be seen?"

So the Caring Cloud asked other caring clouds for help.

They agreed
to be on "standby"
so there would
always be
a caring cloud
in the sky.

And they agreed
to be always
"on duty"
even when
the sun
was so bright,
they were
out of sight.

There was now
a plan
so that
the creatures
of skies,
land,
and oceans
could always
believe
in the Caring Cloud.

The Caring Cloud
reminded
each cloud that
Believing
in Caring
is just the *Beginning*.

"Always believe that *someone* cares about *you,*

And then,

Always have a plan to care for *others.*"

What Are You Thinking About?

What is your favorite part of this story? Why?

What do you think about the Caring Cloud's friends?

What Are You Feeling?

What do you like about clouds?

What will you remember about this story?

What Do You Wonder About?

Do you wonder about why the Caring Cloud cares so much?

Do you wonder where (or why) clouds sometimes hide from our view?

The Flutterby

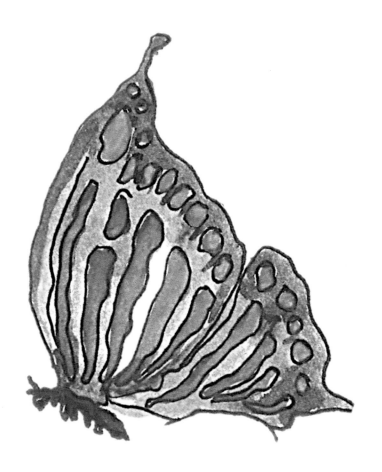

Story by Jed Griswold

Illustrations by Jerry Aissis

Once upon a time,
there lived
two caterpillars ...

Who were
very good friends.

One, named Cat

the other, named Pillar

Not only
did they look alike,
they shared
a common dream.

They both
dreamed of flying.

One day,
they noticed
the dream
butterfly,
fluttering by
high in the sky.

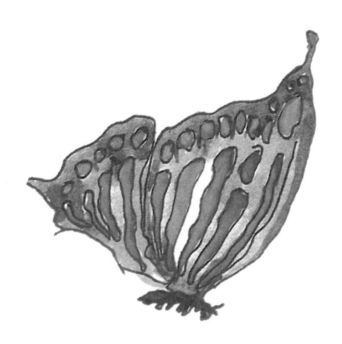

Cat quickly said,
"One day
I will fly, too,
like *that* flutterby."

Pillar made fun of Cat because of the mixed up name for a butterfly.

Then Pillar pondered
for a moment.

"How silly
can you be
to believe
that a creature
of land ...

... could *ever* become
a creature
of the sky?
Just like
fish can't fly!"

But Cat,
the *flutterby-to-be,*
held on tightly
to an important
belief...

that a chance to fly
would one day come by.

"One day,
I will *flutter* by
from flower
to flower,
and fly high
up in the sky."

But there was
a problem.

Neither
Cat nor Pillar
knew how
they could
learn to fly.

So, Cat,
the believing
Caterpillar,
began a search
for advice.

The search began with caterpillar friends.

but none of them
had ever flown,
and they had
no advice
to offer.

One day
Cat noticed ...

the dream
butterfly
just flew,
close by.

So, Cat decided
to ask,
"Who can
help me
learn
to fly?"

The wise butterfly
answered,

"Someone who has
a similar dream,
and who
knows the work
needed to
make it happen."

Later that day,
Cat noticed
a cocoon
hanging from
a limb
of a favorite tree.

walking up
to the cocoon,
Cat asked,

"Is anyone home?"

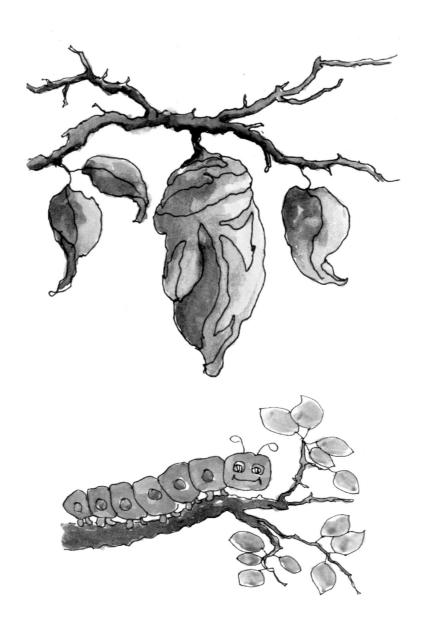

To Cat's surprise,
an answer came.

It was
a soft
and muffled voice,
but Cat
could hear it.

"I'm glad you asked."

"I understand
who you are *today,*
and I also
understand
who you want to be
tomorrow."

Then,
after a pause,
the voice
Continued ...

"Lots of work
has to be done ...

To make sure
your dream is won."

The lessons
began right away.

And Cat was
a good student.

While Cat
was learning,
Pillar walked by.

And Pillar announced,

"I shall build my cocoon,

when I have my own wings;

why work hard, building things?"

Cat thought
for a second ...
maybe two ...
and answered,

"I think I shall build
my cocoon right now

even if to fly,
I don't yet know how."

And so it was,
that one caterpillar
waited and waited
and waited.

And the other one
flew and flew
and flew.

What Are You Thinking About?

What is your favorite part of this story? Why?

What do you think about Cat's belief in being able to fly?

What Are You Feeling?

How do you feel about Cat's belief in hard work to make a dream come true?

What will you remember about this story?

What Do You Wonder About?

Do you wonder about what Cat's friends learned from Cat?

Do you wonder what would happen if the story continued?

Made in the USA
Columbia, SC
08 November 2023

93f9b911-d423-4040-90f4-c5314bfa02d0R02